ANIMAL RESCUE CENTER

The Lonely Kitten

ANIMAL
RESCUE CENTER

Other titles in the series:

ANIMAL RESCUE CENTER

The Lonely Kitten

by **TINA NOLAN**

tiger tales

This series is for my riding friend Shelley,
who cares about all animals.

tiger tales

5 River Road, Suite 128, Wilton, CT 06897
Published in the United States 2019
Originally published in Great Britain 2007
by the Little Tiger Group
Text copyright © 2007, 2019 Jenny Oldfield
Interior illustrations copyright © 2019 Artful Doodlers
Cover illustration copyright © 2019 Anna Chernyshova
Images courtesy of www.shutterstock.com
ISBN-13: 978-1-68010-124-9
ISBN-10: 1-68010-124-2
Printed in China
STP/1800/0215/1018

For more insight and activities, visit us at www.tigertalesbooks.com

Contents

ANIMAL MAGIC
RESCUE CENTER

🏠 HOME

💗 ADOPT

✋ FRIEND

MEET THE ANIMALS IN NEED OF A HOME

COOKIE

The sweetest, most affectionate girl ever! Please let her curl up on your lap.

MIDNIGHT

Midnight has just arrived. She needs a quiet home with no children and no other pets.

ROCKY

A beautiful boy wh needs long walks ar a lot of love. Can you give him a home?

 NEWS

HELP US

CONTACT

 DONATE!

DUDLEY

ft, cuddly, and very
atient, Dudley has
e friendliest nature.
ut watch out—he's
ticklish!

MAXWELL

Maxwell is a lovable,
lively hamster who'll
make a great pet.
You know you can't
resist!

OLIVER

Oliver is 12 hands
high and is just right
for a confident young
rider. Could
that be you?

Chapter One

A Busy Saturday

"How do I look?" Ella Harrison asked her friend Annie Brooks. She stood at Annie's door, wearing her new Animal Magic sweatshirt. It was bright red, with a small white-and-gold logo on the front.

"You look … magic!" Annie grinned.

"They came in the mail this morning," Ella explained. "It was Jen's idea—she thought of it after I'd been on the *Tina Sanchez Show* on TV. We've all got one!"

"Cool," Annie sighed.

"Dad says we're really popular at the moment, and our website is getting a lot more traffic than usual. We want to order more sweatshirts and sell them. It'll help raise money for the rescue center. Hey, Holly, stay down!" Ella turned to her lively Border collie puppy, who was jumping up at Annie. "Oops!"

"Too late!" Annie glanced down at the muddy paw prints on her pink-and-white robe. "It's okay—it'll wash off. How are you, Holly? Have you been on a nice walk?" She petted the lively pup.

"Down by the river," Ella explained. "I'm doing obedience training with her, so we go out early every morning before school. Anyway, since today's Saturday and Mom says we'll be extra busy, I came to ask if you'd like to help out in the reception area."

Annie's eyes lit up. "I'll be there in a flash," she promised. "Oh, and Ella…."

"Yep?" Already halfway down the Brooks's driveway, Ella paused.

"Please order an Animal Magic sweatshirt for me. I'll pay with my allowance money."

"Sure thing," Ella replied, putting Holly on the leash and dashing off.

Animal Magic Rescue Center stood next door to Annie's house on Main Street in Crystal Park. It didn't take long for Ella to settle Holly down in the house and make her way across the yard to the reception area, where she found the room already crowded with visitors.

"I read about Cookie the Yorkshire terrier on your website," a woman was telling Heidi Harrison. "I'd like to offer her a home."

Ella's mom smiled brightly. She was wearing her red sweatshirt under her white vet's coat. "Can I take your name and a few other details? Cookie is very popular—two possible owners have already visited her earlier this week."

"Here's Midnight." Jen, Mom's assistant, was showing another woman a black cat who had come into the center only the day before. "You can see how she's licked the fur off her tummy— that's over-grooming due to stress, I'm afraid."

"Poor thing!" the woman muttered. "Will the fur grow back eventually?"

"Oh, yes—definitely," Jen assured her.

Quietly, Ella made her way behind the desk to find her brother, Caleb, printing out an e-mail.

"Take a look at this," he said, grinning.

Ella picked up the printout. "Dear

Animal Magic," she read out loud, "Scott and I saw the New Year feature about you on the *Tina Sanchez Show*, and we wanted to write and tell you how Honey, our retriever, is doing. She's now fully grown and is very loved, with a silky-soft golden coat and beautiful dark brown eyes. She loves her walks with Scott in the park at the back of Oak Grove—all thanks to you! With very best wishes, Ruth Penny."

"What do you think of that?" Caleb asked.

"Cool." Ella blushed and looked up from the e-mail. She remembered Honey so well—how she'd been secretly dumped on their doorstep, abandoned in a cardboard box. She put the printout down on the table. "Mom, what job should I do first?" she asked, breaking into Mom's conversation.

"Groom Dudley, please. His new owner is coming to pick him up at 10 o'clock."

Ella nodded. "Will you please have Annie come to the kennels when she gets here?"

"Will do," Mom replied.

Escaping from the busy reception area, Ella picked up a dog comb and brush from the storeroom and hurried to the kennels. "Hi, Cookie, hi, Rocky!" she greeted the yappy Yorkshire terrier and a big, dark gray dog with floppy ears and sad eyes. She went up to Rocky's door. "Are you wondering how come nobody wants to adopt you?" she said.

"Cookie gets all the attention, doesn't she? That's because she's little and cute."

Rocky lowered his head and gave a short whine.

"I'm not saying you're not cute!" Ella insisted. "You are—you're totally handsome. But not as many people want to give homes to dogs as big as you."

Rocky's long tail wagged slowly. He stared longingly at Ella.

Tearing herself away from him, Ella went along the row of kennels until she came to Dudley.

The long-haired Labrador-cross came quietly to the door. All around, other dogs barked and yapped.

"Okay, Dudley, it's your big day," Ella explained. She went in and began brushing the soft, cream-colored hair on Dudley's chest. "We'll make you look your very best—yes, I know the brush tickles, but you have to stand still and let me groom you!"

"Can I help?" Annie asked, pushing open the door to the kennel unit. She was dressed in jeans, boots, and a sky-blue padded jacket.

Ella nodded. "Dudley's ticklish. Can you hold his collar while I brush him?"

Together, the two girls brushed out every tangle as Dudley wriggled and sighed. When they had finished, he stood up and shook himself.

"You look incredible!" Annie laughed.

"I have to take him to the reception area," Ella told her. "You can give Cookie a quick brush if you'd like."

So Annie unlocked the Yorkie's kennel and began a pamper session. When Ella came back, it was time to take Rocky for his walk.

"See how good he is on the leash?" Ella led Rocky out of a side door and across the yard. She handed him to Annie and slipped into the house, coming back out with an excited Holly.

"I thought Rocky might like some company!" She grinned.

They set off down the narrow trail to the side of the rescue center, letting the two dogs off their leashes as soon as they reached the riverbank. Rocky bounded ahead, with Holly scampering beside him. When they came to the old stone bridge, they waited for Ella and Annie.

"Good dogs!" Ella told them. She patted them, then took a ball out of her jacket pocket. "Watch this, Annie. I've taught Holly to fetch." She threw the ball back along the path.

Holly raced after it and brought it back.

"Woof!" Rocky's deep bark begged the girls to throw again.

This time Annie threw, and it was Rocky who grabbed the ball.

"Rocky's beautiful. How come he ended up at Animal Magic?" she asked.

Ella shrugged. "The dog catcher in Lakewood found him. He was a stray, so they brought him to us."

There were more throws and chases on the way back, until the girls and the dogs were safely in the Animal Magic yard.

"Do you want to come over after lunch and help in the stables?" Ella asked.

Again, Annie nodded eagerly. "I'll see you in an hour."

"See you!" Ella replied, taking Holly inside to clean her paws on a towel and give her a bowl of fresh, cold water.

Chapter Two
The Discovery

The afternoon turned out to be as busy as the morning. When Ella finally finished up at the computer in the reception area, she was exhausted. She and Annie had mucked out the stables where they were housing two ponies, Gypsy and Oliver, brought over by Cathy Brown from Lucky Star Horse Rescue earlier that week. Then the girls had cleaned the litter boxes in the cat area while Caleb had stayed by

the phone, leaving Jen and Mom free
to deal with two new admissions—a
hamster named Maxwell and Piper, a
sleek white greyhound.

Meanwhile, Dad and Holly were out
in his van making deliveries. Ella had
waved and smiled at Holly perched
happily on the passenger seat next to
her dad.

Now it had grown dark, and all was
quiet in the rescue center. Jen had biked
home to Lakewood. Annie had said
good-bye and gone out with her mom
and dad. And Caleb and Mom had
gone over to the house to make dinner,
leaving Ella in charge of ordering
more sweatshirts. "Animal Magic,
Main Street, Crystal Park"—Ella
typed the correct address on the order

form, pressed Send, then turned off the computer. She was about to switch off the lights when the phone rang, and she picked it up.

"Hello, this is Cathy Brown," the voice said.

"Hi, Cathy. This is Ella. Do you want to speak to Mom about Oliver and Gypsy?"

"No, I just need you to pass on a message." The owner of the pony sanctuary sounded as if she was in a hurry.

"Go ahead," Ella said.

"I'm not sure, but I think I've just heard a kitten in distress."

"Whose kitten is it?" Ella asked, ready with pencil and paper. She planned to write down exactly what Cathy told her.

"That's the problem—I'm not sure who it belongs to. I was out fixing the fence at the bottom of one of my fields and I heard it meowing inside a house down the road from me—there were no lights on in the house or any other sign of life."

"You're sure the owners aren't out at the supermarket or something?" *Kitten*, Ella wrote. *Empty house.*

"I'm sure," Cathy replied. "In fact, I know that the people who lived there moved out earlier this week. That's why I was surprised to hear a kitten crying and why I thought I should let you know. I'm afraid I have to go out now—a work thing—otherwise, I'd have taken a look myself."

"Can you please give me the address?"

Ella asked, writing again as Cathy spoke. *32 Willow Road.*

"Like I said, I might be wasting your time, but I'd rather be safe than sorry."

A kitten crying inside a lonely house down a dark road in the middle of winter—this certainly sounded bad. "Thanks, Cathy. I'll tell Mom." She hung up and ran across the yard to find Mom.

Her mom listened carefully, then nodded. She reached for her jacket. "Come on, Ella—let's go take a look!"

The drive to Willow Road took 20 minutes along narrow roads that curved and rose and twisted and turned. Mom's headlights drilled through the darkness, lighting up the stone walls on either side.

"Cathy did warn me that there might be nothing wrong," Ella told her mom.

Mom turned down Willow Road. "Let's hope that's the case," she said quietly. "But meanwhile, we'll check anyway. There's Cathy's place on the right—see the sign by the gate?"

Ella nodded. "She told me the house is farther down the road. Slow down, please, Mom, so I can take a closer look."

The car bumped and shuddered along the dirt road. "I've never been down here before," Mom admitted.

"There's something up ahead!" Ella pointed out. "A gate on the left and an entrance to a farm. Hang on, Mom—this could be it!"

Mom braked and turned onto the side road. Now their headlights revealed a low stone building and a sign on the gatepost that read 32 Willow Road.

"Come on!" Eager as ever, Ella jumped out. Mom pulled a flashlight from her pocket, and together they approached the house. "It looks deserted," Ella whispered.

Mom listened, then agreed. "I don't hear a kitten, do you? Maybe Cathy made a mistake."

They listened again. A strong wind blew through the trees behind the house.

"Did you hear that?" Ella cried. Above the gusting wind she thought she heard a high, meowing cry. It was muffled and faint, but definitely there.

Mom nodded. "Let's go around the back."

Ella ran ahead, stumbling against a rusty tractor parked at the side of the house, then picking her way over a pile of stones and bricks.

"What a mess," Mom muttered as she followed. She shined her flashlight beam around the overgrown yard and the twisted willows growing by a stream.

"Over here, Mom—I've found the back

door." Ella's eyes had grown used to the darkness, and she could now make out an old wooden porch. Once more she stumbled in her hurry to reach the door.

Meow! Meow! There was no mistaking it now—there was a kitten here in this lonely place, and it sounded as if the noise was coming from the porch itself.

Ella found the door handle and pulled

hard. "It's locked!" she told Mom.

Mom shined the flashlight on the lock, then rattled the handle. "We don't want to break in if we can help it," she pointed out.

But the kitten's cries were growing louder and more pitiful. "We can't just leave it here with no one to take care of it," Ella insisted.

Meow! The kitten must have heard their voices. It seemed to be begging them to rescue it.

"There's a window on the side of the porch," Mom told Ella. "It's not quite closed—let me see if I can slide my fingers in and lift the latch … yes, that's it!"

Slowly the window opened, and Mom pushed aside a sheer curtain to shine her beam inside the porch.

Ella saw some empty cardboard boxes

and a pile of yellowing newspapers sitting on top of a bench. Empty milk bottles were scattered across the stone floor.

Meow! Meow! Meow! The kitten's cries were urgent, but still Mom's flashlight beam couldn't locate the poor creature.

"Let me climb in!" Ella begged.

Her mom nodded, then gave her a boost. Ella squeezed through the window and jumped to the floor, knocking over a milk bottle and making it roll as she landed. She peered under the bench, then into a plastic bowl resting on top.

A big pair of eyes stared back at her.

Ella gasped. "There you are!" she whispered. "Mom, can I please have the flashlight?" She took the light and shaded it with her hand to give her just enough light to see. "It's a little tabby kitten!" she reported. "There's nothing in this bowl except soggy newspaper—there are some unopened cans of food under the bench, but nothing to drink. She must be *so* hungry and thirsty!"

"Lift her out," Mom decided. "See if you can unlock the door from the inside. Quickly, Ella. We need to get her back to Animal Magic as soon as we can."

Chapter Three
Meeting Willow

"Well, what do you think?" Dad asked Mom, while Caleb and Ella stood back from the examination table. "It must have been pretty cold back there at the house. Did you rescue her in time?"

Please say yes! Ella crossed her fingers and held her breath. Her mom had tested the shivering kitten's heartbeat and thoroughly examined the inside of her mouth. Now they were waiting anxiously for Mom's verdict.

"She's a tough little thing," Mom told them. "She seems surprisingly healthy after her ordeal."

"Cool!" Caleb took a deep breath. "How old is she?"

"Six to eight weeks—barely weaned from her mother."

"So sweet," Ella said, venturing forward to pet the rescue kitten.

Back at 32 Willow Road, she'd lifted her out of the dirty plastic bowl and handed her through the porch window to Mom. Together they'd taken her to the car, wrapped her in a blanket, and put her safely in a pet carrier for the rough ride back to Crystal Park.

"She's lapped up the water from the dish, so she won't need a rehydration drip," Mom went on. "We'll start her on small amounts of kitten food—Caleb, can you please go get some from the storeroom? Thanks."

"Can I pick her up?" Ella asked.

"Yes. Snuggle her and keep her nice and warm."

So Ella picked up the tiny kitten. She rubbed between her ears, noticing the narrow stripes running across her head. "She looks like a little tiger!" she joked.

"She's definitely loving your cuddles." Dad smiled as the kitten began to purr.

35

"I don't suppose she's had many of those in her short life so far."

"I know. Someone moved out of the house and left her behind—how cruel is that!" Ella knew she shouldn't be surprised by how unkind people could be to their pets, but she always was.

"Well, she needs a name," Mom said calmly. "And since you did the actual rescuing, it's your choice, Ella."

"Hmmm." Ella petted the kitten's soft front paw and smiled at her little pink tongue as she opened her mouth to yawn. "How about Willow?"

"From Willow Road—very appropriate," her dad agreed. "It suits her."

"Meet Willow," Ella announced to Caleb as he came back with the kitten food and put it on the table.

Meow! The kitten smelled the food and wriggled free. Soon she was at the dish, tail in the air, head down, eating happily.

"Caleb, make sure you take a really cute picture of Willow." It was early Sunday morning, and Ella and Caleb were preparing the kitten's details for the website.

"I always take cute pictures!" *Click-click*—Caleb tapped the phone screen and looked at the result. He'd captured Willow with her head tilted to one side, staring straight at the lens. "See!" he exclaimed.

Meow! Willow cried.

"Oh, look—she wants to be cuddled!" Ella picked the kitten up off the counter.

"I'm off to upload the picture to the website," Caleb said. "Then people can read the details and see how sweet she is."

As he dashed off, Ella stayed for a while with Animal Magic's newest resident. "That's our job," she whispered, putting her lips against Willow's soft, warm fur and explaining their next move. "We put your details on our website, and then we match the perfect pet with the perfect owner!"

"'Willow—how sweet is she!'" Ella read the words that Caleb had written for the

Animal Magic website out loud. "'We hope this abandoned kitten won't be lonely for long!'"

"What do you think?" Caleb asked Jen and Ella.

"That's perfect," Jen told him. "And with the picture to go with it, I'm sure it'll do the trick."

Caleb nodded. "How much do you want to bet that we won't keep Willow here for five minutes?"

Jen smiled as she went to open the front door, ready for business. "Yes, she's a little cutie. Hi, Cathy—how are you?"

The pony sanctuary owner had been waiting in her car for the door to open. Now she breezed in, dressed in jeans and stable boots, bringing the smell of stables with her. "I'm fine, thanks.

I was driving by and thought I'd pop in to check on Gypsy and Oliver, and to catch up on the kitten situation."

"Come and take a look!" Ella invited Cathy to check out Caleb's website entry. "We named her Willow. Isn't she adorable?"

Cathy smiled and nodded. "Your mom called early this morning to say you'd rescued the poor little kitten. She may have had a rough start in life, but by the look of things, you plan to make up for it."

"Do you want to come to the cat area and see her?" Ella asked. Usually she was shy with the brisk, no-nonsense sanctuary owner, but today Ella's excitement about the kitten overcame that. "Did Mom tell you where we found Willow?" she chatted on.

Cathy nodded and followed Ella into the cat area. "On the back porch—left there without a second thought about how she would survive," she replied. "It beats me how people can do these things, but you should see the awful condition of some of the ponies who come to me. Often nothing more than bags of bones.... Oh, yes, I see what you mean!" Stopping beside Willow's cage, Cathy leaned forward. "She really is pretty."

"Hello, Cathy," Mom said, coming out of the storeroom to greet their visitor. "I was just about to call you. I was thinking about Willow earlier, and I wondered if the people who moved out of that house left a forwarding address."

Ella frowned. Why did her mom even want to know?

Cathy shook her head. "To tell you the truth, I didn't even know their names. They were a young couple, but they only rented the house, and I hardly ever saw them in the six months they lived there."

"Cool," Ella said quickly. "Then we

don't need to try and trace them."

"Hold on," Mom argued. "There's a chance that these people left Willow behind in the confusion of moving, and they've only just realized what they've done. In which case, they'll be back."

"No way!" Ella protested. She was eager to find a wonderful new home for Willow. "They definitely dumped her on purpose."

Mom frowned. "We can't be sure, Ella. Cathy, do you happen to know the landlord for that house on Willow Road?"

"Yes. His name is Brian Kozlow. Do you want me to give him a call?"

"Please," Mom said. "I think we should be certain that the tenants can't be found before we post Willow's details on our website. Ask him if he has a forwarding address, and whether his tenants owned a tabby kitten."

"Will do," Cathy agreed, smiling kindly at Ella and going out with Mom to check on Gypsy and Oliver.

Chapter Four

A Home for Willow

"We've got another new admission,"
Jen announced to Ella and Caleb later
Sunday morning. "A stray dog without
a collar or identity chip. He's a mixture
of all sorts, probably mostly Westie,
picked up on Arbor Court after a phone
call from Miss Elliot."

"Cool. Did Cathy call us?" Ella asked.
She'd just come back from Annie's field,
where she'd been helping her friend pick
out a stone wedged in Buttercup's shoe.

"Not yet," Jen told her, "unless she used Mom's cell number."

Ella dashed to the kennels, where Mom was settling in the new dog. "Mom, did you hear from Cathy?" she asked.

"No," Mom answered quietly. "Be patient, Ella."

How? Ella wondered, running back into the reception area just in time to hear the phone ring. She darted to pick it up before Jen or Caleb could get there. "Hello, this is Animal Magic Rescue Center," she said breathlessly.

"Hi, Ella, this is Cathy."

"Cool! I mean, hi, Cathy. Do you have any news for us?"

"I finally got a hold of Brian Kozlow," Cathy said. "He's not happy. He told me the couple, whose last name is Nickel, did a moonlight getaway from the house."

"What does that mean?" Ella frowned.

"They left without paying him the rent they owed, and without a forwarding address, so Brian has no way of getting the money out of them."

Ella nodded and gave Caleb a quick thumbs up. "And does Mr. Kozlow know if they had a kitten?"

"He said yes, they did, even though he has a no-pets rule for his tenants. They got one about a week before they took off. When he asked them about it, they said they were only taking care of the kitten for a friend, but he didn't believe them. He said he was glad to get rid of them in the end."

Ella had put the phone on speaker for

Jen and Caleb to hear. They all grinned
as Cathy finished the story.

"Thanks, Cathy, I'll tell Mom," Ella
promised. She put down the phone and
beamed at Caleb. "Now we can get
moving!" she cried. "Let's put Willow on
the website and see how many calls we
get in one afternoon!"

"We had seven calls about Willow, out of
which there are three possible owners."
Caleb was almost as excited as Ella
about their hopes for the abandoned
kitten. He was chatting with their mom
and dad over Sunday dinner.

Dad turned to Ella. "What was wrong
with the other four?"

"Two already own cats, and Mom thinks Willow needs a home where she's the only one. One lives on a main street—too much traffic. The other woman said she'd call back in 10 minutes, but she never did."

"So what about the three who did make the list?" her dad asked, giving Ella a warning look as she let Holly sneak up to the table and beg for scraps.

"Bed, Holly!" Ella said sternly.

The puppy crept back to her basket by the stove.

Caleb gave his dad the details. "Number one—Tom Larsen at Stonybrook Farm. He wants a new farm cat to chase mice."

"And we like the Larsens," Dad said.

"But it'd be a tough life for Willow,"

Ella pointed out. "She'd have to live in the barn, not in the house. She wouldn't really be a pet, would she?"

"So what about number two?" Dad asked Ella.

"Mrs. Wilson," Caleb cut in. "She lives on the far side of Lakewood, which is a long way away, so Ella wasn't too thrilled about her."

Mom smiled at Ella. "I know you want to find a home for Willow close enough for you to go and visit, but that's not always possible."

Ella blushed. "Mrs. Wilson did sound pretty old," she pointed out. "She might not be able to cope with a new kitten."

"And number three?" her dad prompted.

"Jake and Julie Sharpe," she answered quickly. "They're a young couple, and they're new to Crystal Park."

"And where do they live?" Dad asked
with a grin.

"In a beautiful new house on Arbor
Court, which is really quiet with hardly
any traffic!" Ella said with a slow,
satisfied sigh. "And it's just down the
road from here!"

"The Sharpes have arranged to come
and see Willow at 4 o'clock today," Ella
told Annie as they sat on the school bus
on Monday afternoon. They sat side by
side, looking out at the bleak gray fields
on the way home to Crystal Park.

"They sound nice," Annie commented.
Ella nodded. All day at school she'd

found it hard to concentrate, staring out the window and dreaming about how much Willow would love living with the Sharpes. They would give her a soft bed near a warm radiator and buy her a bunch of kitten toys. She would get the best food and probably wear a collar with a small bell, which would jingle wherever she went. When Miss Jennings had taken attendance, Ella hadn't even heard her name.

"Willow must be a special kitten," Annie sighed.

"What makes you say that?" Ella hadn't realized that she'd mentioned Willow's name to Annie at least 20 times that day. "Willow likes chicken-flavored kitten food...Willow has stripes running over her head...Willow's meow is really cute…!"

Annie grinned. "I suppose it's because you rescued her from that house yourself—that's what makes her special. Anyway, can I come and see this adorable kitten before she leaves?"

Ella nodded. "Better be quick. Come over before 4 o'clock."

"Ella, you haven't even met the Sharpes yet," Annie reminded her.

"I know, but…."

"But you've already made up your mind. You want them to have Willow." Annie laughed, getting up from her seat and walking down the aisle as the bus pulled up to their stop.

Annie was cuddling Willow in the
reception area when Julie and Jake
Sharpe walked in.

"I love her!" Annie told Ella, giving
Willow a tickle under the chin.

Meow! The kitten adored the attention.
She'd been at Animal Rescue for fewer
than 48 hours, but she'd already settled
in well.

"She's so friendly," Annie said as
Willow purred.

"Is this Willow?" Julie Sharpe asked
Mom, who'd greeted them from behind
the desk. Julie was in her late twenties,
with short fair hair and dressed in black
leggings and a gray jacket. Her husband,
Jake, stayed in the background, as if to let
people know that having the kitten was
mainly his wife's idea.

Reluctantly, Annie handed Willow to Julie.

For Julie, it was love at first sight. "Oh, she's so pretty! I've never seen anything so cute and adorable!"

Once more, Willow accepted the cuddles. She peeked out from Julie's arms, her blue eyes gleaming, ears pricked.

"Isn't she beautiful, Jake? Just like she was in the photo." Julie showed the kitten to her husband, who nodded and seemed happy if she was happy.

"Good. I'm glad you like her," Mom said. "She's about two months old, and she's had a hard time lately. She was abandoned, so she needs a lot of TLC to make up for it."

"I find that so hard to believe," Julie gasped, taking a tissue from her pocket to blow her nose. "How could anyone be so cruel?"

"At Animal Magic, we microchip and vaccinate all our animals." Mom went through the formal routine while Ella and Annie stood by. "Willow is perfectly healthy despite her ordeal, and I'm sure she'll make a wonderful pet."

"Are there a lot of people who want to adopt her?" Jake asked.

"We've certainly had plenty of interest," Mom admitted.

But you're our first choice! Ella wanted to say. Instead, she showed Annie her crossed fingers. "They seem really nice!" she whispered.

"So, do we have to join the line?" Jake frowned.

"Not necessarily," Mom reassured him. "I'll ask you a few questions, and if the situation seems satisfactory, we can make our decision on the spot."

Julie smiled and held Willow tight.

"You live at 22 Arbor Court?" Mom checked.

Julie nodded. "Well away from Main Street, with open fields at the back of us."

"And have either of you owned pets before?"

"I haven't, but Jake has." Julie turned to her husband. "You had three cats at home when you lived with your parents."

"Yes, so I know the routines." Jake took over from Julie. "Apart from needing to be fed, cats come and go pretty much as they please. And I guess I'll be the one who gets rid of the dead birds and mice."

"Willow won't chase birds," Julie

protested. "Look at her!"

Snuggled in Julie's arms, Willow looked so sweet, as if she wouldn't even hurt a fly.

"Oh, yes, she will, believe me," Mom smiled. "Dealing with dead offerings is part of the cat-owning deal, I'm afraid."

In the background, Ella grimaced. Julie Sharpe had just shown she didn't know much about having a cat as a pet. Would this worry her mom?

"Anyway, if there are any problems, come back to Animal Magic—we're just around the corner, and we're always ready to help," Mom told the Sharpes.

Good! Ella liked the sound of this. It seemed as if her mom hadn't been

bothered. And the more Ella saw of Julie
and Jake, the more sure she was that
they were Willow's perfect owners—
young, lively, and loving.

Mom smiled. "Do you have any
questions?" she asked them.

"No, I don't think so. Does this mean
we can have her?" Julie blew her nose
again and waited for Mom's answer.

Please! Please! Ella begged silently.

Nestled in Julie's arms, Willow
seemed perfectly content.

"Yes," Mom confirmed with a smile.
"We can provide you with kitten food and
a pet basket, and you can take her with
you now if you'd like. And let me say
that we're very grateful to you for offering
Willow a home."

Chapter Five

A Good Week

On Tuesday, the new sweatshirts arrived before Ella left for school, so she set them out on a rack in the reception area next to the flyers on animal care. Then she ran next door to deliver Annie's.

"They're very bright," Annie's mom, Linda, said doubtfully as she hobbled into the room. She was still on crutches from an accident earlier in the month.

"And really warm," Ella told her. "You should have one for when you're better and mucking out Buttercup and Chance."

Mrs. Brooks nodded. "Yes, Ella, you're right—I'll need a medium. Can you ask your mom to put one aside for me?"

Ella skipped back home with the order.

"We make a profit of five dollars every time we sell one." Caleb had done the math. "At this rate, we'll raise a ton of money."

Then on Tuesday evening, Jen managed to find a home for Midnight, the worried black cat. "She's calmed down a lot since she came here," she told the middle-aged man who came to pick her up. "In her last home, stress is what led to her over-grooming, so she needs peace and quiet—no children and no other pets."

"She'll suit me very well," Mr. Howard told Jen. "I lead a quiet life now that I'm retired. And Midnight will be good company, I'm sure."

Ella was happy to see Mr. Howard go off with Midnight. She headed quickly for the computer to take her off the website. "Oops!" she said to Jen as she browsed the pages. "We left Cookie on here by mistake. Should I take her off, too?"

Jen nodded. "And take Piper off while you're at it, please."

Ella hesitated. "Didn't I just see Piper in the kennels?"

"Yes. But a couple came in to see him this morning and decided they'd like to have him. They've already given homes to two other greyhounds. They plan to pay us a series of visits with their other dogs so that Piper can get to know them gradually before they take him home."

"Good idea," Ella agreed. She took the picture of Piper off the site, then shut down the computer and went to help her mom in the small animals unit.

"Come and see Kiki and King," her mom invited. "They're a beautiful pair of harlequins. Your dad brought them in this afternoon."

"Ahh!" Ella smiled at the soft, cuddly rabbits hopping around their cage.

"Where did Dad find them?"

"A girl at the supermarket checkout told him about them. Her neighbor was planning to set them free in the park. Better to bring them here than leave them in the park, so Dad got there just in time."

"My dad's a hero!" Ella grinned. "I want to tell him. Where is he now?"

"In the house, cooking dinner."

Ella scooted off to praise her dad, but as she ran out of the reception area, she bumped right into Julie Sharpe. "Hi!" she said brightly. "How's Willow doing?"

"Fine."

Julie's answer seemed abrupt, and Ella noticed that her eyes were red and swollen, as if she'd been crying. "Mom's in the small animals unit. Do you want to speak to her?"

"Maybe you can help," Julie said with a frown. "I hadn't realized that Willow isn't house-trained yet. I was at work today, and when I came home, I found she'd ignored the litter box and left wet spots all over our new carpet."

"She's only young," Ella pointed out as she led Julie into the reception area. "It'll take a while for her to learn to use the litter box."

"I thought you might have some flyers," Julie explained.

"We've got a lot of fact sheets and

advice," Ella said. She took four flyers from the rack. "They tell you about the best type of cat litter, keeping the tray clean—all that sort of stuff."

Julie nodded. "Thanks. I'll read them and follow their advice. Hopefully, tomorrow the carpets will stay dry."

As Ella showed Julie out and said good-bye, she had an uneasy feeling. "Otherwise, is everything okay?" she called after the visitor.

"Oh, yes, absolutely fine," Julie said again, hurrying away.

Chapter Six

A Worrisome Phone Call

"Still no new home for you, Rocky,"
Ella said as Caleb brought the gentle
giant back from his walk. It was late
on Saturday afternoon—five days
since Willow had been adopted by the
Sharpes—and everyone at Animal Magic
was enjoying another busy weekend.

Rocky hung his head and patiently
allowed Caleb to untangle his leash.

"Someone will want you soon," Ella
promised, patting his broad head.

"They just have to set eyes on you to see what a handsome boy you are!"

"I'm done for the day," Jen announced, emerging from the cat area and taking the keys to her bike lock from a drawer in the reception area. "Your mom is out in the stables, administering wormers to Oliver and Gypsy. Please tell her I'll see her tomorrow."

"'Bye, Jen!" Ella and Caleb called.

Caleb took Rocky over to the kennels while Ella decided to take down all the out-of-date notices from the bulletin board. Just then, there was a knock at the door. "Come in!" she called.

It was Jake Sharpe who poked his head around the door. "Are you still open?" he asked.

"We're open 24 hours a day if it's an emergency," Mom told him, appearing on the porch. "What can we do for you?"

"Well, it's not an emergency," Jake admitted. "It's more of an ongoing problem."

Uh-oh, Ella thought. *I bet Willow is still peeing everywhere.*

"To be honest, Julie is really stressing about this one," Jake confessed, "and she's developed a really bad cold, which is making her feel terrible." He spoke quietly, in a shy voice, and his beige shirt and gray trousers seemed designed to make him fade into the background. "The fact is, Willow has started scratching the furniture while we're out. She's already made a mess of the table in the dining room, and now she's started on the kitchen door."

Mom listened, then nodded. "That's common with young cats, I'm afraid. Have you tried buying her a specially designed scratching post?"

Jake sighed. "No, but I'll look for one on Monday morning. Will Willow grow out of scratching the furniture?"

"Possibly," Mom replied. "But it's something cats do in the wild as a way of exercising their claws and keeping them sharp."

"So no guarantees?" Jake frowned.

"No, but try the scratching post. And make sure Willow has some toys to play with if she gets bored. That might take her mind off scratching the furniture."

"Okay, I'll do that," Jake promised, taking this as his cue to leave.

"And I hope Julie gets better soon," Mom added.

Jake nodded. "Thanks so much for your help—'bye!"

"Thirty degrees." It was Sunday, and Jen read the thermometer out on the porch as she came into the reception area, her face rosy from the bike ride into work. "It's a beautiful clear day, but freezing!"

"No need to tell us," Caleb groaned. "Ella and I took Rocky and Holly for a walk. The air was so cold that we could see our breath."

Dad grinned at them. "Stop complaining. I like this cold, crisp weather. With a bit of luck, we might even get snow."

"Hmm." Ella frowned. "I'd better remind Annie to make sure Buttercup and Chance are wearing their rugs tonight." She was close to the phone when it rang. "Hello, this is Animal Magic Rescue Center."

"Hello, is this Ella? This is Miss Elliot."

"Hi, Miss Elliot." Ella supposed that

the elderly lady wanted to check up on the mare she'd once owned. "I was just talking about Buttercup. Mom's around —would you like to speak to her?"

"No, thank you, dear. It's not Buttercup that I'm calling about." There was a pause before Miss Elliot decided to continue. "I don't want anyone to think that I'm a nosy neighbor, but I've just seen something that I find rather troublesome."

"Does it have something to do with an animal?" Ella asked. Otherwise, why would Miss Elliot call Animal Magic?

"Yes. It's the tabby kitten at number 22."

"Willow!" Ella gasped.

Everyone in the room turned to Ella and waited anxiously to hear what the problem was.

"That's the one," Miss Elliot answered. "I can see the house from my front window, and I'm always up early—before it gets light, as a matter of fact. Well, I was opening my curtains first thing this morning, and I saw the kitten sitting on the front doorstep, meowing to be let in."

"Oh!" Ella cried. "Does that mean Willow had been out all night?"

"I think so, dear. That's why I'm worried. The door was shut tight, and there were no lights on. There was a deep frost everywhere."

"Out all night," Ella repeated. Willow was much too young to be out in such cold weather.

"She looked so lost and lonely," Miss Elliot concluded. "Honestly, my dear, it was pitiful to see."

"All right, let's take this slowly." As usual, Mom wanted to think the problem through. "We shouldn't jump to the wrong conclusion."

"What's to think about?" Caleb wanted to know, while Ella frowned and bit her lip. "The Sharpes locked Willow out of the house when it was freezing. Then they went to bed. How bad is that!"

"On the surface, very bad," Mom agreed. "But maybe they didn't mean to do it. Mistakes happen, you know."

Jen agreed. "Or maybe Miss Elliot got it wrong. It's possible that either Julie or Jake was up early and had let Willow out for five minutes."

But Ella shook her head. "I don't think so. But it just doesn't make any sense. They both seemed so excited to have her…. Maybe they got tired of her peeing everywhere and scratching. She's so little—she could have frozen to death!" Ella looked at the evidence and rapidly changed her mind about the Sharpes. Now she was certain that Animal Magic had sent Willow to the wrong home.

"It's true that Julie and Jake have been asking for advice," Jen acknowledged. "And Willow has been more work than they'd expected."

"Which proves that they're not used to owning a pet but that they're willing to learn," Mom pointed out. "I don't think we can condemn them for making one mistake."

"A big mistake!" Caleb insisted.

Mom nodded. "But still, I would rather keep an eye on things and not do anything too hasty. If it turns out that the Sharpes are deliberately

leaving Willow out overnight, then
I'm definitely prepared to talk to them
about how dangerous that could be."

Ella and Caleb knew that their mom
had spoken her last word on the subject.
As Mom returned to the morning's
business, they went to the kennels and
admitted how they felt.

"I know Mom wants to wait and see,"
Caleb muttered, "but one more night
like last night could mean the end for
Willow!"

"Don't say that!" Ella cried. A picture
of the beautiful little kitten shivering in
the frosty night entered her head and
refused to go away. "Caleb, we were
wrong about the Sharpes. We made a
terrible mistake!" Ella felt guilty and
angry at the same time.

Leading Piper out of the kennels, Caleb agreed. "So what are we going to do?"

Ella thought hard. On the one hand, do nothing, as her Mom had suggested. On the other, act in secret and save Willow before it was too late. "I'm going to Arbor Court," she decided.

"Just be careful," Caleb warned as he set out with Piper. "Don't rush over there and do something careless."

"Okay, okay," she muttered. "But I don't care how I do it—I'm going to find out the truth!"

Chapter Seven

Trouble!

As Ella set off for Willow's new home, a light snow began to fall. She looked up at the dark gray sky, tied her scarf tightly under her chin, then strode on along Main Street.

"Hi, Ella." It was Caleb's friend George Stevens who slowed her down. "Tell Caleb to come to my house this afternoon. There's going to be a lot more snow. We're making a huge snowman at the top of Three Oaks Road."

More snow? Ella groaned as she turned onto Arbor Court. Normally, she'd have been enjoying the snow with George and his friends, but today she was more worried about the freezing temperature and the effect it would have on Willow. She walked quickly past Miss Elliot's house, crossed the street, and headed for number 22.

No car parked outside the house, she thought as she approached the driveway. *So at least one of the Sharpes must be out. No lights on, so they're probably both out.*

"Yoo-hoo, Ella!" Miss Elliot had come to her front door and was calling across the road. "Have you come about the kitten?"

Ella backtracked. "Hi, Miss Elliot. Yes, I was worried about Willow. I told Mom, but she thinks we should wait a while before we do anything."

"Really?" Miss Elliot sounded
surprised. She bent down to pick up her
elderly cat, Tigger, to stop him from
venturing out of the house. "Why did
your mom think that?"

Ella frowned and felt embarrassed.
"Oh, it's not because she didn't believe
you, Miss Elliot. But she wants to give
the Sharpes a second chance."

"She does?" Miss Elliot raised her eyebrows.

"Yes. Mom says it's possible they left Willow out by mistake."

"By mistake! Oh, I don't think so, dear." Miss Elliot suddenly sounded very firm. "If it had been a mistake, they wouldn't have done it again."

"Again?" It was Ella's turn to sound surprised as she looked anxiously across the street at number 22.

"And so soon. My dear, I've been keeping a close eye on that house ever since I called you. And guess what—that young couple didn't open the door to let the kitten in until after breakfast. I was relieved, of course. But then, shortly after they let her inside, they put her out again."

"What do you mean?" Ella asked.

Miss Elliot looked right at her. "They went out in the car at about 10 o'clock. But before they drove off, they made sure to shoo the kitten out into the front yard and lock the door on her."

"Here, Willow!" Ella searched the frozen flower beds in the Sharpes' front yard. Now she didn't care what anyone said—after what Miss Elliot had just told her, she knew she had to rescue the kitten.

She called again, then spotted tiny, faint paw prints in the snow. They led from the front doorstep around the side of the house.

Quickly, Ella followed them. "Willow!" she called again, scared that the fast-falling snow would cover up the only clue the kitten had left. She reached the backyard and saw a stack of cardboard packaging leaning against the fence. "Willow, where are you?" she called softly.

By now, the paw prints had almost disappeared under fresh snow. Ella could just see that they were heading for the stack of cardboard, so she made her way there, gently lifting the flattened boxes to peer behind them.

Meow! With a terrified cry, Willow shot out from behind the sheets of cardboard.

"Willow, it's me—Ella!"

Meow! Meow! The frightened kitten

cowered on the back doorstep.

Ella was down on her knees, trying to coax Willow to come to her, when the Sharpes' car returned. She heard the engine stop and doors open and then slam. There wasn't enough time for her to find a hiding place. *How am I going to explain this?* she thought, picturing the Sharpes' faces when they discovered her in their snowy backyard.

She froze, listening to the key turning in the front door, feeling the soft snowflakes land on her cold forehead and cheeks. After a short while, the back door opened.

"Willow, here's your breakfast!" Jake Sharpe called. He rattled a dish of dry cat food to tempt the kitten back into the house. Then he saw Ella.

"Hey!" he muttered. "Julie, there's an intruder in our backyard!"

Chapter Eight

A Tricky Situation

In spite of the cold, Ella felt her face flush bright red as she stood in Jake and Julie Sharpe's kitchen watching Willow eat.

The moment the kitten had heard Jake rattle the dish, she'd shot between his legs into the house. Julie had joined her husband at the kitchen door and asked Ella to come in and explain.

"I was worried about Willow," Ella stammered. "She's too little to be out in the snow, so I was trying to catch her before she froze."

Julie frowned. "How did you know she was outside?"

Don't mention Miss Elliot! Ella knew she shouldn't involve the elderly lady. "I was just passing by, and I thought I heard meowing."

"We'd only gone to the pharmacy." Julie was angry. "We weren't out long. Willow would have been just fine," she sniffled, blowing her nose.

Ella nodded unhappily. "I'm sorry."

"That's okay. Don't be too hard on Ella," Jake told Julie. "She couldn't know how soon we'd be back. And she was obviously worried about Willow."

"Well, she doesn't need to be. *We're* her owners now."

"I'm sorry." Ella knew that if Julie was

angry enough to call Mom, she'd be in big trouble back home.

"Time for you to take that medicine and put your feet up," Jake suggested to his wife after an awkward silence. "And time for you to go, Ella." He led her down the hall toward the front door.

"I realize we're not doing very well with Willow," he confided quietly as she stepped out onto the driveway. "It's much more difficult than we expected. Moving is a stressful time, plus Julie is a perfectionist. She hates messes. And on top of everything, she hasn't been feeling very well."

Ella nodded slowly. *So why get a pet?* she wondered. *Pets equal stray hairs and muddy feet. Pets are messy.*

"We'll try harder from now on, I

promise," Jake said.

She wanted to believe him. "And you won't leave her out again?"

"No," he said, before firmly closing the door.

Ella went home and worried all day. She worried about Willow all that evening, and after she went to bed, she lay awake, worrying.

"Where are you now, Willow?" she whispered, staring out her bedroom window at the starlit sky.

She thought back over the day. By lunchtime the snow clouds had cleared, and Caleb had spent the afternoon with George, building the giant snowman at the top of Three Oaks Road. Ella had stayed at home and missed all the fun.

"Are you all right?" her dad had asked. "Or is something bothering you?"

"I'm fine," Ella had lied.

But now, she couldn't sleep. She sat up in bed, pulled back the curtains, and gazed out the window. She saw the pale full moon shining on a white world of snow-covered hills and a sleeping town. And she hoped with all her heart that Willow wasn't out in the white wilderness, but instead safely snuggled up in a soft bed in the warm kitchen of 22 Arbor Court.

Chapter Nine
A Secret Plan

At school the next day, Ella tried hard to concentrate. But every time her teacher told her to do something, her mind drifted off to the problem of Willow.

At least it's not snowing, she told herself, looking out at a clear blue sky.

"Ella, did you hear me?" Miss Jennings asked from the front of the classroom. "I asked you to take this message to the front office."

It's sunny, but it's still freezing, she thought, standing out in the playground with Annie during lunch.

"Hello? Do you want me to help with the ponies when we get home?" Annie asked. "Honestly, Ella, I've said it three times. What's wrong with you today?"

The day dragged until at last Ella sat on the bus, still in a world of her own.

"So tell me!" Annie insisted.

"It's Willow," Ella confessed. The story tumbled out. "New home ... the Sharpes ... out all night ... a terrible mistake!"

Annie listened carefully. "I get it," she muttered. "You think that if you wait too long before your mom decides to step in, it might be too late."

Ella gulped, then nodded. "But I messed up yesterday. Jake and Julie caught me trespassing in their backyard. I'm scared they'll tell Mom."

"And she'd be really angry." Annie understood the problem. She thought for a while. "Maybe we should go undercover."

"You mean like spies, rescuing Willow in secret?" Ella's glum face began to light up. "You think we should kidnap her?"

"Catnap!" Annie said. The bus pulled into Crystal Park, and everyone got off. "We could go to Arbor Court and start right now."

Without stopping to think, Ella agreed, and she and Annie clambered off the bus. "If the house is empty and Willow has been left outside all day, it means that Jake didn't keep his promise," she said. "Which means we have to do something!"

"Catnap her," Annie said again. "Act casual, Ella, as if we're just coming down here to take a walk."

They paused outside Miss Elliot's house, pretending to gossip but really taking a sneaky look at number 22. There was no sign of life, until all of a sudden, a car turned off Main Street into the cul-de-sac.

"It's the Sharpes' car! Quick, follow me," Ella hissed, bolting through Miss Elliot's gate and knocking at her door.

The elderly lady soon appeared. "Ella, Annie, how nice to see you!" she exclaimed. "Come in out of the cold."

"Good thinking," Annie muttered to Ella as five minutes later, they sat in Miss Elliot's living room with milk and cookies. From here they'd had a good view of Julie Sharpe getting out of her car and going into the house.

Ella nodded. "Let's stay as long as we can," she whispered.

Miss Elliot's cat, Tigger, rubbed against

her legs, then jumped onto her lap.

"Is there any more news about the kitten?" Miss Elliot asked, noticing that Ella was studying the goings-on at number 22.

"Not today," Ella replied, seeing Julie come out to unload some groceries from the car. There was no sign of Willow. Another five minutes went by before the front door flew open again. This time, Julie appeared carrying the little kitten at arm's length. Willow hung like a scrap of fur from her hands, legs dangling.

Ella jumped up, sending Tigger sliding to the floor. "It's happening again!"

Miss Elliot, Annie, and Ella rushed to the window to see Julie dump Willow on the doorstep and close the door, leaving her meowing to be let back in.

"Poor thing!" Miss Elliot said with
a shake of her head. "I'd adopt her
myself, but Tigger wouldn't like it. He's
been an only cat for much too long."

"Here comes Mr. Sharpe!" Annie
warned as she spotted Jake walking

toward the house, briefcase in hand.

He immediately spotted Willow and bent down to rub the top of her head. Then he scooped her up and took her inside. But a few moments later, he reappeared with a cat basket.

"What's he doing now?" Ella demanded, so mad that she was ready to rush out and confront Jake Sharpe.

Miss Elliot tried to calm her. "Now Mrs. Sharpe has joined them. Her eyes are red. She looks upset. Oh, dear!"

Jake and Julie seemed to be arguing. Jake had Willow in the basket and was opening the car door. Julie was in the driver's seat, wiping her eyes.

"He's getting in—they're driving away!" Annie cried.

"Where are they going? What are

they doing?" Ella couldn't wait any longer. She rushed to Miss Elliot's front door and ran into the yard—just in time to see Julie reverse out of their driveway and pull away.

Chapter Ten

An Unexpected Turn

"Oh, no, what now?" Ella felt rooted to the spot. In her mind's eye she saw Jake and Julie Sharpe driving out of town into the countryside, choosing a deserted place and stopping the car to dump their unwanted kitten.

"This is awful," Annie groaned as she joined Ella on the pavement. "If only we had a car, we could follow them."

Miss Elliot had stopped to put on her coat. Now she came out of the house, shaking her head.

Annie turned to Ella, flustered. "What do we do?"

"We have to get back to Animal Magic," Ella decided. "I'll be able to look up the Sharpes' cell phone number there. Then Jen or Mom can try to call them."

The girls said good-bye to Miss Elliot and sprinted to Main Street. "Please don't let us be too late!" Ella gasped as she and Annie ran until they came to the rescue center. She was so worried that at first she didn't notice the car parked in the yard.

"Ella, wait!" Annie grabbed her arm and pointed to the Sharpes' car. "They didn't drive off with Willow—they brought her back here!"

In the reception area, Mom and Jen listened patiently to Julie's tearful account.

"I'm so sorry," she wept. "I've brought Willow back. I love her dearly, but I can't keep her."

Ella and Annie were quiet as they came through the door. Jake Sharpe glanced over his shoulder and gave them an apologetic smile.

"I'm so, so sorry, Willow!" Julie cried.

"And in spite of what you might think, it doesn't have anything to do with her peeing on the carpets and scratching the furniture." Jake stood up for Julie.

"It turns out that I have a severe cat allergy," Julie explained through her tears. "I got up this morning, and I could hardly breathe. My eyes were streaming. So I went to see my doctor. He confirmed that I didn't have a cold but was having a serious allergic reaction to Willow."

Jake put his arm around his wife and took up the explanation. "Obviously, we didn't want to leave Willow outside on Saturday, but Julie was finding it so hard to breathe—it was as if she was having an asthma attack—and we both panicked. But then yesterday we got some medicine at the pharmacy, and she felt a little better. She wanted to try again. Then this morning, she felt even worse and decided to see the doctor. He advised us not to keep Willow."

I never expected this! Ella thought, going up to the counter and lifting Willow out of the cat basket. The kitten was shaking. "Shh," Ella soothed.

"Take Willow into the cat area," Mom told her. She turned back to Julie. "It's okay," she said kindly. "You didn't know you were allergic."

"Julie has never lived in a house where there's been a cat before," Jake explained.

"You did the right thing," Mom said. "And don't worry about Willow."

Julie dried her tears. "She'll go to a good home?"

Mom nodded. "Of course. And until that special person finds her, we'll take good care of her here."

"I want to spend a ton of time with Willow!" Ella announced the minute she'd come home from school the next day.

After she'd dropped off her school bag in the house, said hi to Holly, and played with her for 10 minutes, she'd hurried to the cat area.

Jen agreed that the lonely kitten needed plenty of attention. "At the moment, she's a bit wary of people—not surprising after what she's been through."

"I'll take her to the reception area," Ella decided. "It'll do her good to be around people."

She took Willow from her cage and carried her to the busy reception area, where Cathy Brown happened to have stopped by to talk to Mom and Caleb.

"I saw Rocky on your website," Cathy said. "I was browsing—getting ideas for my own website which I plan to set up—and the picture of Rocky hit me between the eyes. He's a handsome fellow."

Caleb nodded. "Rocky's wonderful."

"He might be just what I need," Cathy admitted. "I'm isolated out at Lucky Star. I could use a good guard dog."

Ella tickled Willow's tummy. "You hear that? If Rocky goes with Cathy, it'll be cool."

Mom made a suggestion. "Cathy,
I know it's dark, but would you like
Caleb to take you and Rocky along
Main Street so you can get a look at
how good he is on the leash?"

Quickly agreeing, Cathy waited for
Caleb to bring Rocky from the kennels.

"By the way," she told Ella as she watched her play with Willow. "Seeing the kitten reminds me—I was down in my field this morning, finishing the repairs to my fence, when I saw someone in the yard at 32 Willow Road. I thought it must be a new tenant, but when I bumped into Brian Kozlow, he told me he hasn't found anyone for the house yet. So I'm still on my own down the road, except for the ponies, of course."

"And maybe Rocky!" Ella smiled at Cathy as Caleb came back with a happy-looking dog. "He loves walks," Ella explained to Willow as Rocky went off with Cathy and Caleb. "And I think Cathy likes him, so fingers crossed…."

It was only later, when she was in bed, that Ella thought again about what Cathy had mentioned.

So who was in the yard at the house on Willow Road? she wondered. *Why would anybody be snooping around unless he or she wanted to rent the place?*

The clock ticked on her bedside table, and a bright moon shone through the gap in her curtains.

Maybe the old tenants came back for Willow, she thought. *But then again, why would they? The Nickels definitely didn't want her, or else they wouldn't have dumped her on the porch. Anyway, stop thinking about it and go to sleep!*

But the clock ticked, and Ella stayed awake.

Wait a sec—what did Mr. Kozlow tell

Cathy about his no-cats rule? He said he thought the Nickels had lied and told him they were taking care of Willow for a friend. But what if they weren't lying? What if they were telling the truth?

Ella sat up in bed. "Willow's owner came back to get her!" she breathed. "But when she got to the house, it was empty, and Willow was gone!"

Chapter Eleven
Going Home

"Tom Larsen still wants to have Willow up at Stonybrook Farm," Dad told Ella when she came home from school the next day. "He saw her back on the website and says he'll stop in tomorrow afternoon."

All day, Ella had been in a fever of what-ifs and buts. *What if Willow's owner really did come back? But maybe he or she isn't a good owner. Either way, I have to find out.* Ella had been in such a hurry to get back home that she'd left the books she needed for her homework in her locker at school.

"Dad, can we ask Mr. Larsen to wait a while?" she asked now.

Dad gave his daughter a quizzical look. "Why?" he asked.

"I want to call Mr. Kozlow," she said, deliberately keeping it vague.

Her dad thought for a while, then smiled. "More detective work? Okay, Ella, go ahead. You've got 24 hours."

With fumbling fingers, Ella dialed the number. "Hello, Mr. Kozlow? This is Ella Harrison from Animal Magic…."

"Well?" Ella's dad asked when she got off the phone. He'd watched her face change from a frown to a smile and back again. "Was it good news or not?"

"Mr. Kozlow said that a woman did call him this morning to ask what had happened to the Nickels."

"The old tenants at 32 Willow Road?"

Ella nodded. "Mr. Kozlow told her that they'd left without giving him a forwarding address. But Dad, I think the woman might be Willow's real owner!" And she raced on and explained her brainstorm from the night before.

"Slow down!" Dad begged. "Take me back to the conversation you just had with Mr. Kozlow. Did this mystery woman leave a name?"

Ella sighed and shook her head. "That's the problem," she confessed.

"She talked to Mr. Kozlow, then hung up without telling him who she was."

"It's so sad," Ella said to Willow when she went to the cat area to take her out of her cage. She pulled up a stool and put the kitten on her lap. "There's a woman out there who I'm sure is looking for you, but there's no way I can find out who she is!"

Willow snuggled against Ella's warm sweatshirt. She looked up at Ella with her sweet striped face.

"So even if she is your real owner, you'll probably go to live with the Larsens," Ella went on. "They're very nice, I promise, but you'll have to chase mice and work hard when you grow up."

Meow! Willow sat on her haunches and reached up to paw the gold logo on Ella's sweatshirt.

Suddenly, Caleb burst into the cat area. "Guess what!" he said. "Cathy just called to say she's been thinking about it all day, and she's finally decided to take Rocky. She's on her way right now."

"Awesome!" Scooping up Willow, Ella rushed to the reception area, where she waited eagerly with Mom for Cathy to arrive.

Caleb soon reappeared with an excited Rocky, who wagged his long tail and padded on his big paws around the waiting area.

At last Cathy's truck pulled up in

the yard. "Here she is—and she's got someone with her," Caleb reported from the porch. He held the door open for Cathy and her companion.

"Hey, Rocky—that's my boy!" Cathy smiled as he recognized her from the previous day. Rocky hurried to greet her with a low woof and an extra-big wag of his tail. "Ella, Heidi, Caleb—this is Lucy, and I think you'll be very happy to meet her!"

Ella smiled at the young stranger who stood in the doorway. The dark-haired woman wore a patterned sweater, jeans, and fur-lined boots. At first Ella thought the visitor was staring at her, but then she realized that Lucy's gaze was fixed on Willow.

"Lucy knocked on my door just as

I was leaving to come here," Cathy explained as she petted Rocky and showered him with attention. "Over to you, Lucy," she said with a smile.

"I've been handing out these flyers at all the houses around town." The woman showed them a pile of papers.

Ella took one and read it. "Lost— tabby kitten, eight weeks old. Reward." She read it again, just to make sure. "You're Willow's owner!" she cried.

Lucy Martin's story made perfect sense.

"My dad got sick. He lives in Nevada, and I had to go and take care of him," she told Ella, Mom, and Caleb. "It was very sudden. I'd just moved into the Crystal Park area—Danny and Karen Nickel were the only people I'd met, and they agreed to take care of my new kitten at the last minute. I had no idea they were about to skip town. As soon as Dad was well enough for me to leave, I called Karen, and she said that they'd had to leave their house in a big hurry. She told me they'd left Pixie on the back porch with plenty of food and water. But when I came back to get her, she'd disappeared. And I've been trying to find her ever since."

"Pixie—is that Willow's real name?"
It felt strange to Ella to hand the kitten
over to Lucy. She had a lump in her
throat and tried hard not to let her
feelings show.

"Yes. I'd only had her for a few
days before I left." Lucy smiled as she
took Willow. "I like the name Willow,
though. I think I might change it."

"That would be nice, for Ella's sake,"
Cathy said. "Ella's the one who saved
Willow's life." And she told Lucy the
entire story. "There was no food in the
dish, and the temperature outside was
pretty low. But Ella never gives up on an
animal in trouble," she concluded.

"Then I'll definitely call her Willow
as a way of saying thank you!" Lucy

promised, with a warm smile at Ella.
"Plus, I'll donate the reward money to
Animal Magic. And I'll leave you my
address so you can come and visit her
anytime you'd like."

Willow and Lucy Martin had left the
rescue center in Cathy's car. The last
glimpse Ella had of the kitten was of
her snuggled in a blanket inside a pet
carrier that Mom had provided. She
looked warm and happy—glad to be
going home at last.

"'Bye, Rocky," Caleb muttered as
Cathy let him jump up into the back of
her truck.

"'Bye, Willow," Ella sighed.

She, Caleb and Mom had been joined by Dad and Holly. Together they watched the red lights on the back of Cathy's truck disappear down Main Street.

"Great job, everyone," Mom said as they stood in the dimly lit yard.

"Yes," Dad agreed. "It was great detective work on Ella's part. And thank goodness Lucy showed up when she did! But we'll have to let poor Tom Larsen know…."

Caleb sighed, then picked up a stick and threw it. "Fetch!" he told Holly.

The puppy ran and neatly caught the stick. Everyone clapped.

"Good job, Holly!" Ella cried. "We'll teach you a bunch of new tricks and enter you into competitions and train you to be the best sheepdog in the country, if not the entire world!"

Dad laughed, putting his arm around Ella's shoulder. "And if Ella's teaching you, you probably will be!"

Have you read...

ANIMAL RESCUE CENTER

The Injured Fox Kit

Available now!

by TINA NOLAN

Have you read...

ANIMAL
RESCUE CENTER

The
Porch
Puppy

Available
now!

by TINA NOLAN

Have you read...

ANIMAL
+ RESCUE CENTER

The
Abandoned
Hamster

Availal
now!

by TINA NOLAN